PEDRO

PEDRO'S BIG
GOAL

by Fran Manushkin

illustrated by
Tammie Lyon

PICTURE WINDOW BOOKS
a capstone imprint

Pedro is published by Picture Window Books,
a Capstone Imprint
1710 Roe Crest Drive
North Mankato, Minnesota 56003
www.mycapstone.com

Text © 2017 Fran Manushkin
Illustrations © 2017 Picture Window Books

Library of Congress Cataloging-in-Publication Data

Names: Manushkin, Fran, author. | Lyon, Tammie, illustrator.
Title: Pedro's big goal / by Fran Manushkin; [illustrator, Tammie Lyon].
Description: North Mankato, Minnesota: Picture Window Books, a Capstone
  imprint, 2016. | ?2017 | Series: Pedro | Summary: Pedro would love to be
  the goalie in the team's first game, but another boy is bigger—so all his friends
  come over to help him practice before the tryout.
Identifiers: LCCN 2015046882| ISBN 9781515800866 (library binding) | ISBN
  9781515800903 (pbk.) | ISBN 9781515800941 (ebook (pdf))
Subjects: LCSH: Hispanic Americans—Juvenile fiction. | Soccer goalkeepers—
  Juvenile fiction. | Teamwork (Sports)—Juvenile fiction. Friendship—Juvenile
  fiction. | CYAC: Hispanic Americans—Fiction. | Soccer—Fiction. | Teamwork
  (Sports)—Fiction. | Friendship—Fiction.
Classification: LCC PZ7.M3195 Pci 2016 | DDC 813.54—dc23
LC record available at http://lccn.loc.gov/2015046882

Designers: Aruna Rangarajan and Tracy McCabe
Design Elements: Shutterstock

Photo Credits:
Greg Holch, pg. 26
Tammie Lyon, pg. 26

Printed and bound in the United States of America.
010791R

Table of Contents

Chapter 1
Goalie Tryouts

Pedro didn't like soccer.

He LOVED soccer. He loved running and kicking and jumping.

"Our team is the best!"

he bragged. "Hurray for the

Jumping Wildcats."

Katie Woo cheered too.

"We run fast. We jump high.

We kick hard!"

Coach Rush said, "Next week, I'm picking a goalie for our first game. Who wants to try out?"

"Me! Me! Me!" yelled
everyone.

"Forget it!" sneered Roddy.
"I'm the biggest. Nobody can
beat me."

"Roddy's right," said Pedro.

"He will be the best."

"I'm not so sure," said

Katie. "Bigger is not always

better."

Katie and JoJo and Barry
went home with Pedro to
practice.

Katie kicked the ball to Pedro.

WHOOSH! It went past him.

"Try again!" yelled Barry.

He kicked the ball to Pedro.

WHOOSH! Pedro missed again.

Chapter 2
Practice and Poop

Pedro told his dad, "Maybe I can't move fast enough to be a goalie."

"Don't give up!" said his dad.

"Okay," agreed Pedro. "I'll keep trying."

"I want to play too," said

Pedro's brother, Paco.

"Watch out!" Pedro yelled.

He blocked Paco from

jumping into a pile of puppy

poop.

"Good block!" said Pedro's dad.

He kicked the ball to Pedro. Pedro almost blocked it.

"Keep trying," said his dad. "You will get better."

The next day, Pedro's
friends came over to play.
Barry kicked the ball.

Oops! He kicked it too
hard, and the ball flew over
the fence.

"Arf!" Pedro's puppy, Peppy, chased the ball. He tried to jump over the fence and into the street!

Pedro jumped high. He

blocked Peppy!

"Wow!" cheered Barry. "That

was the best block of all."

"I'll say!" Pedro smiled,

hugging Peppy tight.

Pedro kept on
practicing.

"I wonder who
the coach will
pick to be goalie?"
asked Katie.

"Maybe it
will be Roddy,"
said JoJo.

"Maybe not,"
said Barry.

Chapter 3
The Wildcats' Goalie

Finally, the day came for the tryouts. Katie went first. She missed both balls.

"Better luck next time," said Coach Rush.

Then it was JoJo's turn.

She blocked one ball, but she

missed the next one.

"Not bad," said Coach

Rush. "Let's see who can block

both balls."

"It's my turn," yelled Roddy.

"I know I will win."

But Roddy was so busy

bragging he missed both balls.

Then it was Pedro's turn.

Roddy kicked the first ball.

Pedro blocked it!

Roddy kicked the second

ball. Pedro jumped.

He blocked that one too!

"You win!" yelled Coach Rush. "Pedro is our goalie."

"Yay!" cheered Pedro's friends. "We knew you could do it."

"Now I know too," said Pedro. "I get a big kick out of this game."

He smiled all the way home.

About the Author

Fran Manushkin is the author
of many popular picture books,
including *Happy in Our Skin*; *Baby,
Come Out!*; *Latkes and Applesauce:
A Hanukkah Story*; *The Tushy
Book*; *The Belly Book*; and *Big Girl
Panties*. Fran writes on her beloved
Mac computer in New York City, without the
help of her two naughty cats, Chaim and Goldy.

About the Illustrator

Tammie Lyon began her love for
drawing at a young age while
sitting at the kitchen table with
her dad. She continued her love
of art and eventually attended
the Columbus College of Art
and Design, where she earned
a bachelor's degree in fine art. After a brief
career as a professional ballet dancer, she decided
to devote herself full-time to illustration. Today she
lives with her husband, Lee, in Cincinnati, Ohio.
Her dogs, Gus and Dudley, keep her company as she
works in her studio.

Glossary

bragged (BRAGD)—talked about how good you are at something

cheered (CHIHRD)—shouted encouragement or approval

goalie (GOH-lee)—someone who guards the goal in soccer to keep the other team from scoring

sneered (SNIHRD)—smiled in a hateful or rude way

tryout (TRY-out)—a test to see if a person is able to do something such as play on a team

Let's Talk

1. Pedro loves soccer. What is your favorite sport? What do you like about it?

2. Pedro practiced a lot to get ready for the goalie tryouts. Why is it important to practice? How would the story have been different if he hadn't practiced?

3. Roddy said no one could beat him and he was going to be the best. How do you think that made Pedro feel?

Let's Write

1. Pedro's parents and friends helped him practice to be a goalie. Write about a time you helped a friend.

2. Pedro's soccer team name is the Jumping Wildcats. Write down the names of your favorite sports teams.

3. Draw a picture of yourself playing your favorite sport. Write a paragraph about why you like it.

JOKE AROUND

⚽ Why do soccer players get good grades?
They're always using their heads!

⚽ What do you call a soccer player made of swiss cheese?
a holey goalie

⚽ What did one soccer shoe say to the other?
"Between us, we're gonna have a ball!"

⚽ Why is a soccer stadium the coolest place in the world?
Because it's full of fans.

WITH PEDRO!

⚽ What did the bumble bee say
when it kicked the soccer ball?
"Hive scored!"

⚽ Why did the soccer ball quit
the team?
It was tired of getting
kicked around.

⚽ Why was Cinderella thrown off
the soccer team?
Because she ran away
from the ball.

THE FUN DOESN'T STOP HERE!

Discover more at www.capstonekids.com

- ⚽ Videos & Contests
- ⚽ Games & Puzzles
- ⚽ Friends & Favorites
- ⚽ Authors & Illustrators

Find cool websites and more books like this one at www.facthound.com. Just type in the Book ID: 9781515800866 and you're ready to go!